Quentin Blake

ANGEL PAVEMENT

RED FOX

To all my friends who like drawing

You can find out all about Quentin Blake on
www.quentinblake.com

ANGEL PAVEMENT
A RED FOX BOOK 0 099 45154 9

First published in Great Britain by Jonathan Cape,
an imprint of Random House Children's Books

Jonathan Cape edition published 2004
Red Fox edition published 2005

1 3 5 7 9 10 8 6 4 2

Copyright © Quentin Blake, 2004

Red Fox Books are published by Random House Children's Books,
61–63 Uxbridge Road, London W5 5SA,
a division of The Random House Group Ltd,
in Australia by Random House Australia (Pty) Ltd,
20 Alfred Street, Milsons Point, Sydney, NSW 2061, Australia,
in New Zealand by Random House New Zealand Ltd,
18 Poland Road, Glenfield, Auckland 10, New Zealand,
and in South Africa by Random House (Pty) Ltd,
Endulini, 5A Jubilee Road, Parktown 2193, South Africa

THE RANDOM HOUSE GROUP Limited Reg. No. 954009
www.kidsatrandomhouse.co.uk

A CIP catalogue record for this book is available from the British Library.

Printed in China

This story is about two girls called Loopy and Corky.
They were unusual, and on the next page you will see why.

They were unusual because they were angels.
Most people didn't know that, because in
real life their wings don't show up. But this
is a picture book, so you can see them.

Loopy and Corky hardly knew they were angels, because in every other way they were just like us.

They liked chocolate biscuits. Loopy could put a whole one in her mouth at once.

They liked fizzy drinks. Corky could drink so much that her eyes whizzed round like Catherine wheels.

Sometimes they would have an argument,
and Corky would scream at Loopy.

And then Loopy would scream back.

And sometimes they would scream together,
just for the sheer pleasure of it.

So you see they were perfectly normal girls.

They also both liked drawing.
   They had all kinds of crayons,
      chalks, pens and markers that they had collected
         from people's dustbins and wastepaper baskets.

They drew on old
wrapping paper, wallpaper,
wastepaper: any kind of paper.
They drew for hours on end.

Loopy was very good at drawing soldiers in uniform and people with toothache.

Corky was very good at drawing dogs and birds with lovely tails.

It was because they liked drawing that they thought they would go and see Sid Bunkin, the pavement artist.

He had just finished a cheerful picture of a laughing cavalier, but he didn't look very happy himself.

'Tomorrow is the Big Drawing
Competition, but there's no way
the judges are going to see my pictures.
It's hopeless for a pavement artist…

'Either people walk over your
pictures on their way home…
or it rains and they're all
washed into the gutter.

'And if you lift up the paving stones
you get into trouble.'

'I know what,' said Corky. 'We can give you a special pencil from our collection. It draws in the air and it's absolutely heavenly.'

'Simply angelic,' said Loopy.

'Totally divine,' said Corky.

'You still have to know how to draw, though.'

Sid Bunkin had a go with Loopy and Corky's pencil.
It really did draw in the air.
　　He drew a fish...

...and two birds...

...and an acrobat.

Then Loopy and Corky grabbed him by the braces and off they went, up and up like a helicopter over the town.

They went past the new building site...

...and over the old traffic bridge.

They went past the
Town Clock Tower...

the Griswold
Building...

Filbert's
Department
Store...

and St Simeon's Church.

They went over the Brick Street school playground…

...and the Sunset Retirement Home.

The Big Drawing Competition was in Prospect Park.
All their friends were there – George and Jo
and Dave and Gigs, Big Rob and Little Zip
– and lots of other people.

They had never seen
drawings in the air before
– it was just amazing!

Then the judges gave the prizes.

There were prizes for drawing animals and birds…

…portraits of your family…

…monsters…

…and where you spent your holidays.

Sid Bunkin was awarded the prize for the best
surprise drawing.

Everyone clapped and cheered, especially Loopy
and Corky and their friends.

Next morning, Sid Bunkin
went back to working on the
pavement with the best quality
Artist's Pastels which were
part of his drawing prize.

But later on in the day,
when there were not many
people about, he took
the special pencil from
behind his left ear.

This time – can you believe it – the drawings took
to the air on their own, even though Sid Bunkin
stayed just where he was.

Up and up they went, all over the town.
It was extraordinary.
 But then, when you start drawing you can
never be quite sure what is going to happen
next, can you?